The KISS BOX

by **Bonnie Verburg**
illustrated by **Henry Cole**

ORCHARD BOOKS • NEW YORK
An Imprint of Scholastic Inc.

Bonnie Verburg wishes to thank
Dianne Hess, her extraordinary editor,
and Kathy Westray, art director and designer beyond compare.

Text copyright © 2011 by Bonnie Verburg
Illustrations copyright © 2011 by Henry Cole

All rights reserved. Published by Orchard Books, an imprint of Scholastic Inc.,
Publishers since 1920. ORCHARD BOOKS and design are registered trademarks
of Watts Publishing Group, Ltd., used under license. SCHOLASTIC and associated
logos are trademarks and/or registered trademarks of Scholastic Inc.

Library of Congress Cataloging-in-Publication Data
Verburg, Bonnie.
The kiss box / by Bonnie Verburg; illustrations by Henry Cole.—1st ed.
p. cm.
Summary: As they prepare for a short separation, Mama Bear and Little Bear
find a way to reassure each other while they are apart.
ISBN 978-0-545-11284-0 (reinforced bdg. for library use)
[1. Mother and child—Fiction. 2. Separation anxiety—Fiction. 3. Bears—Fiction.]
I. Cole, Henry, 1955- ill. II. Title. PZ7.V58258Ki 2011   [E] — dc22
2009012102
10 9 8 7 6 5 4 3 2   11 12 13 14 15   Printed in Singapore   46
First edition, December 2011
Henry Cole's artwork was rendered in watercolor and colored pencil
on Arches Hot Press watercolor paper.
Book design by Kathleen Westray

For Robert Martin, with love

—B.V.

With many thanks

to my friend Nancy

—H.C.

MAMA BEAR was always home,
and that's how Little Bear liked it.
But sooner or later, all mama
bears need to go away, even if
it's just for a little while.

"I'll be back soon," Mama Bear
promised. "Let's have fun today—
before it's time to say good-bye."

But Little Bear did

not want to say good-bye.

"I miss you already," he said.

And his mama said, "I miss you, too."

"Will you come back?" Little Bear asked.

"I will always come back," Mama Bear told him.

"And even
when I'm
not with you, Little Bear, I'll send you love and kisses
every minute of every day. Just like I'm doing now.

Can you feel them,

flying through the air from me to you?"

"Yes," said Little Bear. "But are you sure you won't forget me when you are gone?"

"I will think about you all the time," said his mama, "no matter where I am or what I do."

"Even when you are very busy?" asked Little Bear.

"No matter how busy I am, you are always *most* important," Mama Bear said, and kissed his ears. "You know that, don't you?"

"I do," said Little Bear, "but I want you to stay home."

"I can't stay home," said Mama Bear. "But I can leave you a hundred kisses to keep you company. And every time you miss me, you will have *all* those kisses. Do you remember how to count to one hundred?"

"I do," said Little Bear. "But where will I keep your kisses so they don't get lost?"

Mama Bear smiled. "I will give you a special jar," she said. "And I will fill it with a hundred kisses.

Every time you need a kiss, just open the jar,

and a kiss will fly from me to you."

"But what if I break the jar, Mama?"

"Then I will fill an envelope with a hundred kisses. And every time you need a kiss, just open up the envelope, and a kiss will fly from me to you."

"But what if I lose the envelope, Mama?" asked Little Bear.

"Then I will kiss your fingertips with a hundred kisses. And every time you need a kiss, just touch your fingers to your heart, and a kiss will fly from me to you."

Mama smiled. "You won't lose your fingertips, will you, Little Bear?"

"Oh, no, Mama," said Little Bear. "But how can I send my kisses back to you?"

Suddenly Little Bear had a good idea. "*I* know how I can send you kisses, Mama. Then we can always be together."

"How?" his mama asked.

"It's a secret!" said Little Bear. "Don't peek!"

Little Bear found a small box. He drew a picture of himself and glued it inside. Then he filled the box with a hundred kisses, every one as special as the love he felt for Mama Bear.

When Little Bear finished, he called
out to his mama:

"*SURPRISE!*

Here is a kiss box for you! Now
you make one for *me*."

"What a smart little bear
you are," said his mama.

"Will you help me make it?"

"Yes," said Little Bear.

Now Mama Bear and Little Bear

each have a kiss box of their own.

And whenever they are apart,
they keep their kiss boxes close.

Do you know why?

So they can send kisses back and forth,

no matter where they are.

Together or apart,

their love goes on and on . . .

. . . just as ours does

each time we say

I love you

with a kiss.

STORYTELLER'S NOTE

WHEN MY SON was very young, his godparents, Audrey and Don Wood, gave him a remarkable gift. It was a green ceramic and metal jar, and Audrey explained that it was a "kiss jar." Whenever my son and I were apart, we could use it to send kisses to each other, and no matter how many kisses we took out of the jar, it would always remain full.

Over years of use, the kiss jar became dented and worn, but Audrey was right—it never ran out of kisses. Then, when my son was eleven, we were separated for half the summer while he journeyed with his dad to another country. The kiss jar was too big for the trip. So I found a small wooden box, the size of my thumb, and put a postage-stamp-size photo of myself inside—and on tiny sheets of paper I wrote out the words in this book. The night before he left, I surprised him with it and read him the story.

Throughout his childhood, my son and I found the kiss jar enormously comforting. And when he was older, his long trip away was made easier for me because the kiss box was with him. Wise Audrey and Don Wood knew that kiss jars and boxes are sometimes just as important to mama bears as they are to the little bears we miss.

A kiss box can be made of anything at all—from a simple container you make yourself, to a treasured family item. The only thing that is essential is a good imagination . . . and an abundance of love, of course.